hello
genius™

DUCK GOES POTTY

BY MICHAEL DAHL   ILLUSTRATED BY ORIOL VIDAL

PICTURE WINDOW BOOKS
a capstone imprint

Duck wears

DIAPERS.

One day, his mommy says,

"M
DIA

"You're a **BIG** DUCK now."

The first time,
DUCK MISSES.

The second time,

The third time,

Now, when Duck has to go, he sits on the potty chair

ALL BY HIMSELF.

"Remember to wash your feathers," says Mommy.

"You're a **BIG**

DU

hello genius

Hello Genius are published by Picture Window Books – a capstone imprint

1710 Roe Crest Drive, North Mankato, Minnesota 56003

www.capstonepub.com Copyright © 2010 by Picture Window Books. All rights reserved. No part of this publication
may be reproduced in whole or in part, or stored in a retrieval system, or transmitted in any form or by any means,
electronic, mechanical, photocopying, recording, or otherwise, without written permission of the publisher.

Library of Congress Cataloging-in-Publication data is available on the Library of Congress website.
ISBN: 978-1-4048-5726-1 (board book)   978-1-4048-7119-9 (board book)
978-1-4795-2126-5 (e-book)   978-1-5158-0429-1 (saddle stitch)

Designer: Bob Lentz
Creative Director: Heather Kindseth

Printed and bound in China.
009805